AMY REDEK
HOT EROTICA

No
WHITE
Snow

WARNING

This book contains sexually explicit scenes and adult language. It may be considered offensive to some readers. This book is for sale to adults ONLY.

* * * * * * * * * * * * * * * * * * *

Please store your files wisely where they cannot be accessed by underage readers.

Please feel free to send me an email. Just know that these emails are filtered by my publisher. Good news is always welcome.

Amy Redek - **amy_redek@awesomeauthors.org**

You might also want to check my blog for Updates and interesting info.
http://amy-redek.awesomeauthors.org/

About the Publisher

4Fun Publishing, a member of **BLVNP Incorporated**, 340 S. Lemon #6200, Walnut CA 91789, info@blvnp.com / legal@blvnp.com
NOTE: Due to the highly emotional reaction of some people to works of erotic fiction, any email sent to the above address that contains foul language or religious references is automatically deleted by our anti-spam software and will not be seen. All other communications are welcome.

DISCLAIMER

Please don't be stupid and kill yourself. This book is a work of FICTION. Do not try any new sexual practice that you find in this book. It is fiction and not to be confused with reality. Neither the author nor the publisher or its associates assume any responsibility for any loss, injury, death or legal consequences resulting from acting on the contents in this book. Every character in this book is over 18 years of age. The author's opinions are not to be construed as the opinions of the publisher. The material in this book is for entertainment purposes ONLY. Enjoy.

No White Snow

Hot Erotica

By: Amy Redek

ISBN: 978-1-68030-008-6

My name, though of no consequence, is Julie Winters and the younger sister of April, though her surname has now been Summers after marrying Jack, who is now my brother-in-law. How and why she married a man with that surname considering what hers had been, I never had the gall to ask her.

They had been married for almost two years. During the first year, my mother died; and after another year, my father followed her. I was then seventeen years old and since there was no will written by my father, the house and any monies in the bank etc., were then passed onto both my sister and myself.

Rather than living on my own, my sister suggested that I live in her house while we sell our parents' house. This way, we could have a bit of money each. Since I still had a year of college education and being virtually broke, I agreed to her suggestion, and so I moved in, though for that first year, I spent most of my time at the college and it wasn't until I got my diploma, did I really move in to live with my sister and brother-in-law.

I didn't know then of the desire that Jack had for me, but later found out after living with them for three months. April had gone up north to see how an aging aunt was coping, I was left alone with Jack, who told me to stop calling him brother and use his name.

That first night, we were alone, he suggested that instead of me cooking dinner, we go out for that evening meal. He was the perfect gentleman then and after a lovely meal, we returned home and he suggested that we have a couple of drinks before bedtime. I'd already had half a bottle of wine and thought that a couple more drinks would be okay, so I said that it would be a nice way to round off the evening.

Now I can't say if he spiked my drinks or not, but a lot of what happened, I cannot really remember. I know I laughed a lot as we had our drinks and must have been given some kind of drug for when he pulled me into his arms as we sat on the sofa, I had no objection to him kissing me. I must have liked it, with him really being the first man to kiss me and didn't even have any qualms about having his hand fondling my breasts as we kissed.

Nor did I object when his hand went inside my blouse and had it push up my bra to release my breasts and have his hand massage them. Nor did I stop him from taking off my blouse and bra for him to kiss and nibble on my nipples. I think I enjoyed it since I stroked his hair as he sucked on my nipples and didn't stop his hand from wandering down over my stomach and moved down under the waist of my skirt to have his fingers enter my pussy.

I appeared to have enjoyed his fingers playing with me for I gave out a little cry when he pulled his hand out and didn't see him pull down the zipper of his trousers because he was still kissing me. He then took hold of my hand and guided it into his trouser that was now open. He pushed my hand inside till I felt his erection and had him curl my fingers round that hard muscle of flesh and gently moved my hand up and down on it.

There is a gap in what I remember for the next thing I know, we were lying on the rug and I was no longer wearing my skirt but completely naked as he was. He was down in between my legs and had his tongue moving about in my pussy, licking and sucking on me. His tongue was also exciting my clit. I gave out a cry when he stopped doing that to me as it was really exciting me. He then started kissing my stomach first before slowly moving up, kissing me all the way until he was kissing and sucking on my breasts.

It was when he moved further up my body did I then feel the head of his cock enter me, rubbing against my clit as his tongue had done before he pushed his cock further inside me. He was, by then, kissing me on the lips when he broke through my hymen and was the first man to do so; turning me from a girl into a woman.

I felt a short, sharp pain that was quickly dismissed as he filled me with his hard cock. I felt it really throbbing away as he then had his erection fully inside me, our pubes meeting when he could go no further. He was still kissing me as he lifted himself up onto his elbows and then began to move his cock back and forth inside me.

I think I was then somewhat in a delirious state, for my arms went round his back and my legs seemed to have lifted of their own accord as he fucked me. His lips left mine as he lifted his head up as he really began to plough himself into my virgin meadow and had him cum inside me, gasping as he did so. His body then came back down on top of me, squashing my breasts with his chest and kissed my neck, feeling his hot breath as well as feeling his cock still throbbing away inside me.

We lay like this, joined together for several minutes before he lifted himself up and felt his cock start to slide out of me. When out, his hands came up under my arms and he lifted the top half of me upright and moved me round so that I was leaning back against the sofa.

He straddled my body as he moved closer, his still hard cock waving in front of me, my eyes mesmerised at seeing what had just been up inside me, shining with both of our juices.

'Open your mouth, Julie,' he said, which I did, and had him lean in closer and had the head pushed inside. It was hot and rubbery and I could feel and taste both his cum and my own juices with my tongue.

'Suck and clean it,' he said, his voice sounding as though he was miles away, and I did as I was told. Having it still throbbing away while I did as he told me, sucking, licking and almost chewing on the hard piece of flesh that I had in my mouth.

I don't really know if I enjoyed it or not, for the next thing I could remember was being helped up the stairs as he put me into my bed.

I woke up in the morning feeling ghastly and with a pounding headache, a sore mouth and an itching pussy. I only had the vaguest memories of what had happened the night before and felt disgusted that I had let Jack fuck me as I struggled out of bed go to the bathroom. I made it just in time as I could feel the bile coming up into my throat and just as I made it to the toilet pan, I fell down onto my knees and threw up.

With my stomach then empty, I got up by the basin and rinsed my mouth before sitting down on the toilet for a pee before flushing that and my vomit away and went into the shower. I only felt a mild bit better after that, drying myself and putting on a dressing gown, still having this throbbing headache. I made my way downstairs and into the kitchen where the medical cabinet was and got out and swallowed some Aspirins before putting the kettle on for some coffee to really wake me up.

I staggered out into the dining room, a misnomer for it was really part of the open lounge, with a table, four chairs and a cabinet there. Jack came into the lounge, he too, was just wearing a dressing gown.

'You look ghastly,' he said, looking at me.

'I feel it too,' I replied. 'I don't know if it's what I had to eat or drink, or…or what happened last night.'

'Well I enjoyed last night, didn't you?' he said with a big smile on his face. 'Would you like to do it again?'

'No. All I want is a cup of coffee and then go back to bed,' I told him, and upon hearing the kettle bubbling away, I went back and made two cups of coffee, leaving one on the table for him, took mine back upstairs and got back into bed to drink my coffee before going back to sleep.

~~***~~

It was late afternoon before I woke up again, feeling much better, only having a slight throbbing in my head, which another two tablets would soon make it disappear. I had gotten dressed before going back downstairs and saw that Jack was watching the news on the television.

'You won't tell April what happened last night, will you?' I asked, standing in front of the television screen to get his attention.

'Good lord, no!' he exclaimed. 'She'd kill me and kick you out, but I would die a happy man with what we had together last night.'

'Bully for you, for I don't remember much of it,' I said.

And that was the only time that I had sex with him, for April returned soon after this conversation, which made it impossible though I wouldn't have him fuck me again anyway.

~~***~~

Winter was approaching fast and I got an invite to a party organized by those students that had been at the college the same time as me. I had a taxi take me there and I had a good time. When it came to an end, I was offered a lift home, which I accepted. Whether this was a mistake or not, I don't know.

We were moving down past a local forest, with this fellow driving, when he started running a hand up and down my leg. I kept pushing it away until I could take no more of him doing this, especially when his hand came up under my skirt.

'For fuck's sake!' I cried. 'That's enough. I'd rather walk home,' and pulled the hand brake up hard, making the car swerve about on the road before it screeched to a stop. I quickly had the door open and got out. 'Now fuck off,' I shouted at him before slamming the door and moving off down a small path that led into the forest.

I was only in it for a few minutes, thinking that he might follow me and so turned off and moved farther into the forest. Needless to say, I got lost. It was dark in there and I just kept stumbling on. My skirt got caught several times on some bushes, tearing it; and I began to get frightened at what else might happen whilst in there.

I soon found out, well not really then, but later. In my stumbling about in the dark, I tripped over something and fell head-first into a muddy puddle, hitting my head on a fallen branch and passed out. I learned later that I had lain there all night in this muddy water and almost died of hypothermia since it was so cold there.

I had been found in the morning, covered in mud and shaking with the cold and in a coma. I was carried to a cottage that wasn't far from where I had fallen and was washed and put into a small bed and watched over for three days until I came out from that coma and found a small man sitting there next to me.

'Thank heavens that you've woken up at last for we've been most anxious for you,' he said, his hand felt my brow. 'At least your temperature feels normal now. We've been worried sick that you might die on us.'

'Who's we and where am I?' I managed to croak out.

'My brothers and I and you are here in our winter cottage,' he said. 'You were absolutely filthy, covered in mud and soaking wet when you were found. So we carried you here where I washed you and got you into this bed and put as many covers as we could over you as well as some hot water bottles that we kept putting in with you. I've even been giving you sips of soup, praying that you would eventually come round, which thank the lord that you have.'

'How long have I been here?' I again croaked out.

'Three days and nights,' he said, and moved over to where there was a small oil-burning stove that had a saucepan on it. He poured some of what was inside into a cup and brought it over and lifted up my head, putting the cup to my lips and found that it was some kind of soup that was being given to me. Hot as it was, I swallowed all of it before he laid my head back down onto the pillow to refill the cup and gave me some more of that soup.

'This is better than keeping your mouth open and pouring it in, making you cough before swallowing it,' he said smiling at me. I thought he was sitting down as he said this but then realised that he was standing up.

'You're small for a man,' I said before realising that I was being rather rude.

'That's because I am a dwarf,' he said. 'We all are.'

'I'm sorry I asked for it was rather rude,' I said without a croak this time after having my throat cleared by the soup.

'No need to apologise,' he chuckled, 'We're used to being called funny names.'

'You've used the word we several times now. Who's we?' I asked.

'My brothers. Seven of us and we're all dwarves, me being the eldest,' he said.

'Shades of heaven!' I exclaimed. 'Would that make me Snow White?' This brought out a big laugh from him.

'Now that would be the icing on the cake if it were,' he laughed. His laugh was quite melodious and it was a lovely smile he had and it was pleasing to the ear, and I snuggled down a little in the small bed I was lying in.

'Tell me more,' I asked of him.

'Well we are Romany gypsies by birth. My mother and father being just that, though sadly, they died some years ago now. During the summer months, we perform in a circus and this is our winter home. It's not ours really, but we have been given permission to use it as such by the owners of this land. That includes this forest that we live in these past few months,' he told me.

'Are you acting as clowns in the circus?' I asked, only ever having been to one circus.

'Sort of. Though we always go into the ring as the seven dwarves, singing that famous song "Heigh Ho!", he laughed. 'It get's the crowd going for we put on big red noses and dress like the dwarves in the Disney film. Did you know that that was made back in 1937?'

'No, I didn't,' I said.

'Or that the original was written way back by the brothers Grimm?'

'No to that either, though I did read the story when I was a child,' I told him.'

'It would be great for the circus and us if you were to join us and become Snow White in the ring. I can see that it would bring the house down,' he mused, his eyes going all misty.

'It's a nice thought, but I should really be getting home as my aunt and uncle will be worrying themselves sick with me being away so long without them knowing where I am,' I told him.

'You're not fit to go anywhere at the moment. It's going to be a week at least before you would be able to. Though there's nothing wrong with you writing a letter that one of us will post for you while you are recovering,' he said, which made sense as I found out a little later when I did get up from this small bed. I now know why it was so small and wondered who had to give it up for me.

'Well I think I'd better start by getting up from this bed,' I said and then realised that I was naked beneath the bed covers.

'I've got no clothes on!' I wailed.

'You couldn't have been put into this bed with the muddy clothes you were wearing, plus you had to be washed first,' he chuckled. I felt that my face had gone quite red at knowing that one or more had helped get my clothes off and had seen me naked.

'How…how many of your brothers saw me without clothes on?' I stammered.

'Now that was a difficult thing for us to do and there were only three of us though it was only myself that laid hands on you in the washing process. And I must say that you have the most perfect body I have ever seen, and before you ask, I was a gentleman in doing so, and also the only one to help you in, I suppose you would say, your ablutions,' him looking quite contrite in mentioning this bodily function.

'Wh….where are my clothes now?' I asked, blushing.

'All washed and dry, but you are going to need help for you will feel rather weak after being in a coma for three days,' he said shyly.

'Well as you have already seen me without clothes, I will accept your help in getting me dressed,' I told him.

'I'll get………….,' and he told me a name that to me, was unpronounceable, let alone something I can spell, and let it go at that. He went off to the door and shouted out this name, telling him to bring in the washed clothes of mine. While he was there, I looked about the room that I was in and saw that there were another six beds plus the one I was in and wondered who had to sleep somewhere else.

'Whose bed is this?' I asked when he returned to stand by the side of the bed. He told me the same name that I couldn't speak of.

'He's the youngest of us and is a bit on the simple side for there was a problem at his birth and mother died with him coming out into the world. There might have been ten of us if she had lived longer,' he said.

'How long ago was this?' I asked.

'Twenty years ago, so that is his age and I'm now thirty and the oldest one, so I think it was really too much for her body to take. My father died ten years ago which left me to keep the others in line so to speak. It seems to have worked out okay. Ah, here he is,' and saw this youngest of the tribe coming in carrying my clean clothes.

'Is she all right now?' he asked him, using the name which was unpronounceable to me.

'She's just fine,' he said as he took my clothes from him. 'Stay,' he said as the youngest one started to leave, 'and help me get her dressed.' He turned back, his face a bright red as he looked at me still under the bed covers.

I turned to the elder one. 'Look. I can't pronounce either of your names…..'I began and the elder chuckled again.

'That I can understand,' he said, 'so as it was just I who looked after you, you can call me Doc and my brother here is also known by us as Dopey. In fact, for the others I'll let you pick the names that you know from the story,' giving out another chuckle. 'Right. Let's get you dressed. Dopey, move behind and help her to sit up.' This he did by moving out of my sight and had him put his arms down in the bed and under my shoulders and gave out a noise as he lifted my back up. This made the bed cover fall down so that my breasts were exposed to Doc's eyes. It felt as though my face had gone red at him seeing them but then realised that he had seen them more than once as well as the rest of my body. I watched him pick up my bra first and came towards me and I found that I couldn't lift my arms up more than a few inches.

'I can't move my arms,' I cried.

'No matter, life will come back into them soon,' he said as he slipped the straps under my hands and pulled the bra up to settle on my shoulders. 'You'll have to excuse me,' he said as he lifted up one breast first to be able to get it into the cup before seeing to the other one and with a little more of moving them in the cups, pulled the straps round and clipped the two ends together. With the help of Dopey, the next item put on me was my blouse and had it buttoned up at the front. Now came the tricky part. Doc pulled the cover down the rest of the way to reveal the lower part of my body and I blushed even more as he saw my sex right in front of his eyes. It didn't seem to faze him as he then pulled my legs round to the side, making me swivel round and making Dopey move round too, still with my upper half upright. He put my feet through the bottom part of my panties and pulled them up as far as he could.

'Lift Dopey,' he said and I had Dopey behind me give out a grunt as he lifted me just enough for Doc to pull my panties up to my waist. Then he picked up my suspender belt.

The strap that is there should have been put on first,' I told him, realising that I should have told him this before the panties.

'Sorry. I didn't know,' he said. 'This is the first time I've ever done something like this before,' as he put the belt round my waist and held me upright as Dopey then clipped the two ends together behind me.

'The straps now should be on the inside of the panties,' I told him and had him then blushing as he used his hands to get all four straps down through the underside of them.

'These now? he asked, holding up my stockings.

'Yes,' I told him. 'Roll them down until you reach the toe part and you then put my toes inside and roll the stockings up to then be able to fit the clips inside and out. Well you'll see once they are pulled up.'

He had a problem doing this as he could only get both stockings up as far as the middle of my thighs for I was still sitting down on the bed.

'Get on the bed Dopey and lift her so that she can stand up,' he said and I felt Dopey get onto the bed behind me and with more grunting, managed to lift me up for me to sway forward and had Doc brace me from falling forward. I now had Dopey's hands round my waist, holding me upright for a few minutes, me having gone quite dizzy with having my blood suddenly moving down to the lower parts of my body. This settled down and was now standing on my own two feet though I still felt a little wobbly but was held there by Dopey as Doc finally managed to get the stockings clipped into place. It made me smile at the difficulty he had in seeing that the clips were firmly in place.

Lastly came the skirt that I had been wearing and with him lifting each foot in turn, was able to then pull it right up to my waist and fix the thin belt that held it up at my waist.

Doc now was holding round the waist when he got Dopey to get off the bed and stand on one side of me to help Doc in getting me to walk without falling over. It was an effort but with him holding me tight, was able to flip each leg, one at a time, forward, and so we slowly made our way to where the door was.

Doc called out for someone to open the door as we stood a little way back for the door opened inward and this was done by another small man, seeing a big smile on his face at seeing me being held up and so immediately named him Happy.

There were cries of delight with the others seeing me brought into the lounge or sitting room, whichever they called it, me seeing for the first time the brothers. All being roughly of the same size as Doc and Dopey, both of their heads only just coming above my waist line, helping me to cross the room to sit me down in a big comfortable cushioned sofa-style chair.

I was exhausted with just those few steps I had taken and now could see in front of me, my lovely seven dwarves. So I now had Doc one side of me and Dopey on the other.

'I must thank you all, gentlemen, for rescuing me from the forest and in upsetting your winter vacation in looking after me. Now, Doc, here,' and this made them give out titters at me calling him this, 'has told me of his name and that of Dopey,' which brought out more tittering laughs. 'which I'm afraid, I couldn't understand a word of their proper names, let alone to be able to use them, so named them as you are, to me, the seven dwarves that rescued Snow White.'

'Will she be able to sleep upstairs now?' one of those in front of me asked. 'For I'm knackered at having to be out here and not getting much sleep for the past three nights,' and he gave out a big yawn.

'I think I shall call you Sleepy,' I said which brought on more laughter which bolstered me up somewhat. So now we have Doc, Sleepy, Dopey and Happy named, leaving Grumpy, Bashful and Sneezy. The latter was an easy one for one of them sneezed and so was called Sneezy which made them laugh. I looked at the other two and smiled, one went a little red in the face and so called him Bashful.

'This is all very well,' said the last dwarf, 'but let's hope she can cook for I'm fed up with what we've been getting over these past few days.'

'I'll do the cooking for you as soon as I am able, Grumpy,' I said which brought out laughs and some clapping of hands.

'Right on the button,' cried out Doc. 'He's been grumpy ever since he was born,' and so all seven now had a name I could say when speaking to them.

'Well when I'm able to do some cooking for you to show my gratitude in you finding and looking after me, I will also see to what this place looks like,' I said, finding I was able to raise up a hand to sweep it about the room. 'I'm surprised that you haven't realised that the place is like a pig sty. It's filthy, so I will clean it up for you.'

I was later taken upstairs to the single room that was there when I was able to walk by myself, and over the next couple of days, began to do the cooking for them as well as giving the whole place a damn good cleaning. It was on my fourth day of coming out of my coma and having noticed that the upstairs bedroom had a bathroom that had a bath inside that I decided to go further with them.

I was now completely mobile and it was Doc that I collared first.

'When was the last time you had a bath?' I asked of him. His head drooped and he could only murmur that he didn't know.

'Well we'll see to that. Upstairs with you,' I told him and so followed him up and pushed him into the bathroom. I'd learned since I was mobile that the cottage had three fire places, one in the lounge, one in their downstairs bedroom and one in what was now my bedroom. All the fires having logs to burn which the forest was full of, and that each had at the back, a boiler behind which gave the whole cottage a constant supply of hot water.

'Now get undressed,' I told him as I got the right tap working to start filling the bath with hot water, though also adding some cold water till it was good enough to have a bath in and not be scalding.

Doc was now naked and trembling at not only having to get into the bath water but having me see him naked, his hands crossed in front of his male parts.

'Don't be shy, Doc. You've seen me naked and even washed me, so now it's your turn and by jove, you do need it,' I said, pushing him closer to the bath. It was with some trepidation that he got into the water having to use both hands to hold himself up as he slowly sat down. The water almost immediately began to be discoloured but I ignored this and began by washing his hair, really scrubbing it with plenty of soap, him then having to lift his hands up to keep the soap from his eyes.

I saw in the murky water that his cock, flaccid, was almost as big as that of brother-in-law Jack when erect, but ignored it for the moment as I rinsed his hair and carried on in scrubbing his neck and shoulders until the water was too dirty to carry one and so stopped and pulled out the plug.

When the bath was empty, I put the plug back in the hole and turned the taps on again but controlled the outpouring of it so that it wasn't too hot for Doc, whose hands were back down covering his genitals. I turned off the tap when the water level was up to his waist and then lifted each leg up in turn as I washed them plus his feet before getting him to stand up in the bath.

This he did and I then washed those lower parts that had been beneath the surface, washing his thighs and his backside and made him turn round so that I could wash the front of him. My hands soon pushed his hands aside and began to wash his private parts and began to take my time in washing his cock and balls, and in doing so, made his cock start to rise up to the way I was washing it. It wasn't long before his cock was fully erect and sticking well out in front of his groin.

I then had the urge to do what my uncle had made me do to his erect cock, but this time, it was me that wanted to do this and so, really getting the soap suds off his cock, leaned forward over the bath, and with me holding his cock, took the head into my mouth and started sucking on him, pushing the foreskin back to tease the G-string and made him quiver. So much so, that it was almost something instinctive for his hands to come onto my head as I sucked on him, to hold my head there as he couldn't help but let his cum erupt out of his cock and fill my mouth which I moved round as it collected itself together for me to then swallow it.

He had at first groaned when I had taken the head of his cock inside my mouth, but now having given me his cum, gave a big sigh at the release that his balls had needed. I finished sucking on him now that he was empty of his seed, released him and looked at him and smiled.

'I think you likcd that, Doc?' I said. 'That was my way of saying thank you for helping me when I was in need.'

'That I did, princess, but you didn't have to go that far in thanking me for what I did for you,' he said.

My own body beneath the top of the bath was shivering with the delight I had just had in sucking on his big cock and now wanted it up inside me, but would save that for later as there were still six more dwarves that needed a damn good bath.

I got up, keeping my hands from trembling as I helped him out of the bath and began drying him with a towel, just loving to stroke his cock again beneath the towel at the same time.

When he was dried, I told him to go and put on some clean clothes and those that he had worn, to be left downstairs for me to wash later. I also told him to send up another of his brothers to be washed as I ushered him out of the bathroom before starting to fill the bath again. It was already full when I had Happy poke his head inside the doorway.

'I…I was told by Doc to come up here,' he stuttered, and I had to grab his arm to pull him inside to stand him next to the bath.

'Well you look as dirty as he was, and now he is nice and clean, so get those dirty clothes off and get into the bath,' I said in a stern voice. He didn't look at all happy now as he turned his back towards me as he slowly peeled his clothes off and saw that he really did need a bath. Like Doc, his hands were covering his front which made it difficult for him to get into the water, but he managed and sank down, sitting upright as I began by washing his hair first.

That didn't take long and was soon washing his filthy neck and shoulders and soon washed each leg before changing the now dirty water and refilling the bath with clean fresh water. I had to really thump him to stand up for me to wash his back and upper thighs and bum before turning him round to wash the front of him.

By pushing his hands away from his groin, I saw that he was about the same size as Doc and began to wash those parts that he had tried to cover. Again, with the way I handled him and washed him, I had his cock grow up to be a full erection and as with the Doc, I rinsed him off first before pulling him to the edge of the bath and took the head of his lovely rampant cock into my mouth to do the same to him as I had to Doc.

He tasted just as nice and did the same to the others who followed up in turn for me to bathe. The last one to come into the bathroom was Grumpy and straight away lived up to his name.

'I was made to come up here,' he began. 'I only agreed because I was told of what you would do when I was clean, princess,' he said. He wasn't as bashful as Bashful had been, him almost fighting me as I struggled to get his hands off of his erection as I washed him. Grumpy let me see him when his cock was flaccid, but with it now being fully erect, had no compunction in sticking his throbbing cock into my mouth when I opened it.

Though it should have been me taking control of him, it was reversed and had him holding my head in his hands as he then face fucked me, giving out a big sigh as he gave me his cum to taste before swallowing it.

'That was lovely, princess,' he said when I released him, and helped him out of the bath to dry him with the now wet towel that I had there in the bathroom.

'What's with this princess thing?' I asked of him, having all of them calling me that.

'To us, you are a princess in doing what you are doing for us. Getting us clean and putting things to right, such as having you soon to wash our clothes and as you said, cleaning up the place,' he said before wrapping the last towel round himself before leaving the bathroom.

I cleaned the bath from the scum that had been left from having seven of them being washed in it, before I went downstairs to start cooking their dinner.

But before I could do that, I had seven sets of dirty clothes to see to and found that they did at least have a boiler there in the kitchen and so dumped these in first and had the water boiling before I started seeing to their dinner. Rabbit stew, which seemed to be their basic dinner with them catching them in traps in the woods.

I had turned off the boiler, leaving the clothes to soak till the morning before sitting down with them to eat our dinner. I was surprised that they had all waited until I was sitting down too before they began eating. It was only when we had finished our meal did I drop a small bombshell on them.

'Now you all know what I did for you in the bath and for me to say thank you again in having taken me in instead of leaving me out in the woods to die, I would like two of you to share my bed for the night,' I said, looking at the different expressions on their faces, wondering what they all were thinking, for I knew what I wanted. Having seen, felt and sucked on them all, now wanted what brother-in-law Jack had given me, and that was to have their cocks up inside me.

They were sitting there stunned as I got up from the table and went and got seven straws from the kitchen and took them back, sat down and cut two of the straws making them smaller than the others. These I shifted about in my hands under the table before bringing up one hand holding the straws and placing it on the table.

'I think that they should be drawn in order of seniority,' and held my hand to Doc. He pulled out a long straw, his smile disappearing at not pulling out a short one. Happy was happy to pull out the first short straw, chuckling and almost looking at those that lost. Grumpy and Bashful lost, too, in pulling out long straws, leaving Sleepy, Sneezy and Dopey.

The three looked at each other and it was Sleepy's turn and his hand trembled as he pulled one of the three left and was crestfallen when it was a long one. Sneezy rubbed his hands together and gave me a big smile as he pulled one out but found that it was the long one with Dopey then having the only one left, which was revealed as the short one cried out. 'It's not fair! I'm older than he is.'

'It was a fair draw,' Doc said, 'so shut up.'

'So,' I said, getting up from the table. 'So someone else can do the washing up tonight, for I'm going to bed. Are you coming?' I asked, looking pointedly at Happy and Dopey. Both had big grins on their faces and quickly got up from the table and followed me upstairs.

When we were in my bedroom, those two just stood there, not quite knowing what to do and so I started the ball rolling by taking my clothes off for them to see me naked as I got onto the bed, moving into the middle and patted the bed on both sides of me. There was no need for words and they were very quick in getting their clothes off for me to see that the pair of them had full erections, which would have put many men to shame at the size in comparison to their height. They were quickly on the bed and then lay there like dummies. Their hard cocks reaching up past the navel when laid against their stomachs.

'Well there's two of you and I've got two tits, so start by sucking on them,' I said quite firmly and had both of them move down a little and had the pleasure of having both hot mouths begin to suck on my nipples. With both of them doing this, I began to get an itch down below and gave Happy's head a push.

'As I've sucked on your cock, Happy, go down and use your tongue in my pussy and make me happy,' I said, and as Happy moved down and had his tongue start probing in between my legs, Dopey stopped sucking on my nipple to move up and kiss me. With Happy now further down my body, Dopey moved to lay on top of me, his throbbing cook now between my breasts.

'I love you, princess,' he said in between his kisses.

'I love you too, Dopey. Especially where your cock is at the moment,' and had an idea. 'Sit up where you are, keeping your cock where it is.' He gave me a strange look but did as he was told by moving his legs down either side of me and was then sitting on my chest with his big cock between my tits. I put my hands up and squeezed both tight around his cock with just the head peeking out. 'Now start fucking my tits.' He had a bewildered look on his face now but began to move himself on top of me and began moving his cock there, me seeing the head poking out from between them as he moved.

'I'm going to cum all over your face, princess, doing this,' he said.
'Let it go for I want to see your cum shooting out of your lovely cock. What I don't catch in my mouth, you can lick.'

His face turned into a big grin and he really began to move faster, the purple/red head of his cock keep showing itself, the eye winking at me. He now had his hands on his hips as he fucked my tits and gave out a gurgle.

'I'm cumming, princess, I'm cumming,' and saw his first emission come shooting out of his cock, me lifting my head up but only catching half of it in my mouth, the rest splattering on my upper lip and chin. I didn't have time to swallow it as the second load came out, which I caught and had him gurgle again at him seeing this happen and was able to catch the next two as well, the last lot, not as strong as the other emissions, only hitting my chin as he came to a stop, breathing heavily.

I smiled up at him and let him see his cum in my mouth before I swallowed it and had him then pull his cock out from between my tits to lay on top of me to kiss and lick my face that was covered in his cum that missed my mouth. I could feel that I wasn't far from having an orgasm and cried out to Happy to now put his cock up inside and to fuck me. Dopey still had his legs astride me and I now could feel his bum being bumped by Happy's head as his cock smoothly filled me and made me happy too.

Dopey moved off of me so that he could continue licking his cum off my face and I just loved the way Happy was fucking me, having his pulsating cock setting all my nerves on edge as he humped away and it wasn't long before I felt his cum hitting my insides, glad that it was only a few days ago that I'd had my menses and so wouldn't have gotten pregnant with him cumming inside me.

He came to a stop and collapsed on top of me, his face pressed into my chest just below my tits, feeling his hot breath there as he panted away. His cock still throbbing inside me and feeling my inside muscles flexing themselves round his lovely organ, his chest heaving away on my upper stomach. It took him several minutes before he had the strength to lift himself up, a big grin on his face as he looked up to me and slowly moved himself backwards and I felt his cock sliding out of me and when he rolled over onto his back, I was quick to move down the bed and take that wonderful cock of his into my mouth to suck both some of my juices and traces of his cum to savour along with the pleasure he had given me.

Having sucked and licked him clean, moved back up the bed and had them pull the covers up and with them either side of me, we fell asleep with them both sucking on my tits.

~~***~~

On waking up in the morning, I could feel that both of them had an erection and wanted them badly and so had Happy fuck me first and when he'd cum inside me, let Dopey then put his cock inside me while I sucked on Happy's wet cock. It was lovely to have had both of them fuck me with their rampant cocks, feeling their cum shoot out inside me. With Dopey having given me his cum, I had him sit on my chest so that I could suck on his still hard cock and had Happy then tonguing me down below.

I was as happy as Happy in having had the two of them pleasure me and I know damn well from the looks on their faces that they had enjoyed fucking me, but now it was time to get up. So as they got dressed, I went into the bathroom to run the bath water and said to the two of them as they came in and helped in washing me, that there should be a shower in the room, but there wasn't any space left to put one in.

They even helped get me dry when we'd finished with having had my bath and I shooed them out for me to get dressed. They both thanked me for a lovely night and wished that they could do it again one night. With them gone, I started getting dressed, putting on the sorry looking skirt that had rents where it had been caught on some brambles before I fell in the mud. Even my blouse had been torn too. But my skirt suffered some more as I left the bedroom for as I shut the door, part of it got caught and so as I moved away, another piece was torn off of it, almost baring my left leg. Well there was nothing I could do about it, so I carried on downstairs and began to see to getting breakfast for us all.

It was Doc who remarked about the state of my skirt and blouse. 'I think that we should get you some decent clothes,' he said. I started to make objections to them buying me new clothes but he kept hushing me. 'With you already doing what you have done to the place so far, it's the least we could do. I'll run into town with Bashful, he's very good with a needle and thread.' Which didn't mean much to me at the time. 'Is there anything else we can get you?' The first thing that popped into my head was some birth control pills and I'm sure I blushed when I mentioned this. Well by the time I got the last one to fuck me, I would be close to my fertile time and by taking some now would prevent me from ovulating. I also asked if they had any writing paper and an envelope so they could post a letter for me. I then explained that it was for my sister who would be worrying about the fact that I'd been away from home for over a week now, so as to put her mind to rest.

Then it dawned on me that Doc said he would go into town and that was at least two miles away and said that they shouldn't walk that far just for me. He chuckled. 'We don't walk, We've got a car,' he said and that made me wonder what kind of car they had with them being so small and mentioned this. 'We'll show you after breakfast,' he told me.

So before I did the washing up of the breakfast things, also knowing that I had all their clothes in the boiler, left that to go and see this car, following Doc out and round to the back of the house. It was not a car per se, but more of a mini bus and had a surprise when I was shown the inside. The driving seat was very small and much higher than the normal seat of a car. Also that the pedals where built much higher and the gear stick much closer and the steering wheel smaller. He told me that it had been specially made for him to be able to drive it and it would also tow their sleeping trailer when travelling with the circus.

So back in the house, I wrote a short letter to tell my sister that I had fallen ill and was now being looked after by a lovely family of seven and that I would be with them for at least another week or two before I was fit to travel back. Though the following week, I sent another letter saying that I would be staying with them for a bit longer, not giving any date of when I might be leaving them.

We all stood outside the house to wave to both Doc and Bashful when they drove away to go into town and I had also asked them to get some more food and milk etc. Then it was time for me to wash the breakfast things and see to the scrubbing of their clothes that had been in the boiler overnight. I had all these hanging out on a washing line before the van turned up from town.

They had several bags of shopping and a big box, which I was told had some clothes inside for me to wear after it had all been sewn up by Bashful. They had posted my letter and passed over the box of birth control pills and then showed me that they had bought a full length dress for me but it still needed some work being done to it before I could wear it. 'You wouldn't have to wear stocking with this,' Doc said as I held it up to my front. We didn't buy a bra either, but if you need another one, we can get that next week,' he said. I could see by holding the dress up to my front that it needed shortening and there was other pieces still in the box, but they were not handed to me as they would be sewn to the dress later by Bashful.

There had also been some other paraphernalia with them that was quickly carried in by the others and it disappeared with three of them as they took it upstairs. I didn't find out what it was until it was bedtime that night.

After lunch with the clothes being almost dry, I brought them inside and ironed them before giving them back to each of them to put away.It was almost time for dinner, which was a beef stew.

After we have all eaten, and I had some help in washing up before we returned to the table, I had five straws in my hand, two of them shorter than the others. Happy and Dopey could not pick one this time. Doc missed out again by pulling out a long straw as did Sneezy. There was a grunt from Grumpy in pulling out the first short one, but he had a smile on his face in doing so; Bashful drew a long one and it was Sleepy who pulled out the last and second short straw.

'Sorry, boys,' I said to Doc, Sneezy and Bashful.

'I don't mind,' said Bashful, 'for it will give me time to finish sewing your dress tonight, though I hope to pick a short one tomorrow night.'

Like last night, having already seen and sucked on their cocks, I was happy to now have two of them fuck me and took hold of Grumpy and Sleepy's hands and led them upstairs to my bedroom.

'You others can do the washing up,' I called back over my shoulder, and led the two with me, into the bedroom and, like the night before, got undressed first and went and laid down on the bed for them to see me naked, waiting for them to be the same. Sleepy gave out a yawn as he began taking his clothes off.

'Don't you fall asleep now, Sleepy,' I said.

'If he does, I'll take over his share,' Grumpy said with a grin, dropping his trousers for me to see that his cock was sticking up like a barge pole. 'And if it's as good as Happy said, you'll be able to call me Humpy instead of Grumpy.' I couldn't help but smile at that and patted the bed next to me and had him walk over, his cock swaying from side to side as he did so. Mind you, Sleepy's cock was just as big and moved in the same way and I had them both onto the bed on either side of me.

'What else did Happy say?' I asked, not caring which one answered, looking down to see both big cocks resting on their stomachs.

'That you had two tits,' Sleepy said, 'and we were to start by sucking on them.'

They both moved down the bed a little in unison, turning onto their sides and feeling those two lovely cocks press up against my thighs as they both took a nipple each into their mouths to start sucking on them.

'I don't mind nibbling, Grumpy, but not chewing,' I said.

'Sorry,' he mumbled and was then more gentle in what he was doing. I let them mould and squeeze my tits as the sucked on my nipples for a few minutes before I asked, 'Who's going to fuck me first?'

'Me,' said Grumpy, lifting his head up from my tit. 'He might fall asleep before I've finished and then I can do it a second time.'

'Well let's see and feel you start,' I said, and he quickly moved farther down the bed and pushed my legs farther apart and surprised me by going down even farther and sticking his tongue into me first. He found my clit straight away and I couldn't help but give out a groan as he gently nibbled on it in between sticking his tongue into the entrance to my pussy.

'Don't tease me, Grumpy. I want to feel you fully inside me,' I said and had him quickly move up, having his chest up on my stomach as his cock began to slide into me. I could feel it throbbing and almost drooled at having him begin to move that lovely cock of his inside me.

Sleepy was still sucking on my tit as he massaged the other, but oh how I wanted to have his cock in my mouth but held back as I was approaching my orgasm and I could then have him fuck me after Grumpy had cum.

'I'm nearly there, Humpy,' I cried out and had him ramming harder into me and had my whole body shaking and shuddering with my hips moving up to Grumpy's thrusts as I had my orgasm, feeling him cumming inside me at the same time. What bliss at the way that all my body nerves made my body tingle with delight at having both at the same time.

Sleepy let go of the tit he had been sucking and moved up and kissed me.

'I love you, princess,' he breathed into my mouth as he kissed, his lips feeling very soft against mine.

'I love you too, Sleepy, and now, with having Grumpy cum inside me, I want to feel yours doing the same,' I managed to say, and had him move down as I had Grumpy pulling himself out of me, my muscles fighting to hold him there. But he came out and felt him move to one side as Sleepy got between my legs.

'Come up here, Grumpy,' I croaked, 'and let me suck on your lovely cock.' And as he moved up, Sleepy entered me and could feel him really throbbing away and hoped that he would last long enough to give me my second orgasm. Grumpy arrived and straddled my chest and leaned forward having both of his hands on the pillow under my head as the head of his cock brushed against my lips as I opened my mouth to take it in. It was smeared with my juices that I avidly licked off and really squeezed his cock as I moved my hand up and down on it, trying to get any leftovers of his cum to savour and swallow.

I was being thrilled at both ends with Sleepy really ploughing my meadow and me sucking away on Grumpy's still hard cock. It was a maiden's heaven. With my legs up in the air to give Sleepy more room, wondered what it would be like to have a third dwarf with his cock stuck up my ass, being fucked in both holes whilst sucking on another. As there were still three of them to see to me, I thought I would give it a try the next night. The only trouble by having my thoughts wander was that Sleepy began to cum inside me before I had a second orgasm, neither did I get anymore cum out of Grumpy. You can't win them all I realised as Sleepy came to a stop and lay on my stomach, kissing my chest and had Grumpy pull his cock out of my mouth to then kiss me also.

'I love you, princess,' said Grumpy in between kisses.

'I love the pair of you, even more so when you are fucking me,' I said, making sure that Sleepy heard me and gave out a little cry as I felt his still hard cock start to slide out of me. He then moved up the bed and began kissing one of my nipples and then had Grumpy move down the bed to use his tongue inside me. This allowed Sleepy to move further up the bed so that I could suck on his wet cock.

Grumpy was so good in the way his used his tongue and teeth around my clit that I was able to then have my second orgasm, really smothering his face and could hear him slurping away as I licked Sleepy clean.

It was then a happy three that cuddled up to go to sleep. Them, having got their end away in fucking me. And me, fucking them and having had two orgasms.

~~***~~

I woke up feeling a finger inside my pussy, stroking my clit and opened my eyes to see that Sleepy still had his head outside of the bedcovers which meant it was Grumpy down below.

'Use something bigger than a finger, I said to him on pushing the covers down a little way. He looked up at me and grinned as he then moved in between my legs that I opened and had him push his hard throbbing cock up into me. Oh how lovely it was in feeling that hard piece of flesh moving inside me and gave Sleepy a kiss to wake him up as I wanted him to do the same when Grumpy finished cumming inside me. It wasn't long in having Grumpy really pumping himself into me that I began feeling his cum splashing away inside of me, loving the thrill it gave me to feel it coating my vagina.

As he began to move, pulling himself out, Sleepy was quickly down pushing himself into me and had Grumpy come up the bed for me to suck on him. Sleepy didn't last long and was soon shooting his load of cum into me and I then sucked on his cock to lick it clean.

After which, we all got out of bed and went into the bathroom where I got a surprise. With there being a toilet downstairs, I hadn't come up to the one in my bedroom and now knew what was in the bundles that they had carried upstairs yesterday. There at one end of the bath where the taps were, they had fitted a shower and a hanging screen to stop the water from splashing out onto the floor.

'Oh you lovely little men,' I cried.

'That's the best we could do in giving you a shower as there isn't enough room to have a cubicle,' Grumpy said, both him and Sleepy having big grins on their faces at see the pleasurable smile I gave at what they had done for me, and gave them both a kiss before getting into the bath and having a proper shower. They obviously used the toilet for a pee as I heard the pan being flushed, while I had my pee whilst having this shower. I was in there for some time, loving this shower for when I eventually turned it off and got out of the bath to dry myself, they had already left and on entering the bedroom, found that they had gone downstairs.

With me then being down there with them, I thanked them all for what they had done for me and gave them all a kiss before preparing breakfast for us all. After this was eaten, I now always had two in the kitchen to help me in doing the washing of the plates and utensils while one wiped them dry and the other putting them away, so that chore was soon done and on returning to the dining area, saw that they were all sitting there with big grins on their faces.

Wondering why they were still there was soon resolved for Doc stood up as Bashful left the table and came back with the big box that they had brought in the day before.

'This is for you, princess,' Doc said as Bashful placed the box on the table. 'Bashful worked on it and finished it last night.'

'Thank you,' I said as I then opened the box to find a dress inside. I pulled it out and gasped, for it was a replica of what Snow White wore in that wonderful film. It was a white voluminous dress that had a stiff back collar but had a black bodice from the waist up. The sleeves were from the shoulders down to just above the elbow joint and was a puffed up blue with two red designs on them. 'This is beautiful!' I cried, holding up against my front and saw that it was the right size.

'There's this also,' Doc said, passing me a red ribbon that had a bow at the front which would hold my hair in a form of a pony tail. This was perfect as I had black hair, the same as Snow White had.

'Can I put it on now?' I asked. Not to anyone particular, looking at the grinning faces before me.

'Yes, princess,' Dopey cried out.

'Yes, put it on,' the others cried, and so I gathered it up and went upstairs to the bedroom that I occupied at night, though now I was really calling it my bedroom. Inside, I quickly got my almost ragged clothes off and pulled the dress over my head and pulled it down over my naked body. I found that I didn't need to wear a bra either, for the top half had been designed to have space for my breasts.

I brushed my hair at the back so that the ribbon could be under the back part of my hair but still come over to sit on top of my head with the bow at the front. I quickly then left the room without shoes on and I saw at the bottom of the stairs, a pair of white slippers for me to wear, these I slipped on as all seven of them looked at me. They had big smiles on their faces as they looked and Happy was pushed forward to some whispering from the others.

'Er, princess,' he began, almost stuttering. 'We also fixed this to the wall there,' and pointed to where the stairs ended to see that a full length mirror had been fixed to the wall. 'Just look and see how lovely you are.' I really did feel like I was a princess when I saw myself in the big mirror and couldn't help quoting from the story.

'Mirror, mirror on the wall, who is the fairest of them all?' The mirror didn't answer me but all seven of them did in unison.

'You are!' they cried and clapped their hands. I turned to face them, tears in my eyes as I looked at their smiling faces and I went to each one of them and gave them a kiss as I thanked them for this wonderful present.

'You deserve it, princess,' Doc said, being the last one kissed. 'You have brought life to this once filthy house. Cleaning it up as well as us, and we love you for it.'

'Also the decent meals we are now getting,' said Grumpy.

'I like the bed time best,' said Dopey and got a slap from Bashful.

~~***~~

'Well it's time for lunch,' I said.

'I'll do that for you, princess,' Dopey cried out.

'Thank you. That means I can start preparing the evening meal,' I said, getting Sneezy to go out into the garden to get me some carrots and cabbage for the beef casserole that I could then get it into the oven on a low temperature. This gave me time then to write another letter to my sister to say that I would be staying longer with this lovely family. It got posted a few days later.

Time passed on and it was soon time for dinner which they all loved and there wasn't a scrap left afterwards.

'Is it time for bed yet?' Sneezy asked, looking at the clock on the wall. I had noticed that not only him had been clock-watching, but Doc and Bashful too.

'There's the washing up to be done yet,' I told him.

'The others can do this,' Doc said, his eyes alight at knowing that he would soon be fucking me.

'Yes,' cried Bashful.

'Do you want to go to bed now?' I asked, teasing the three whose turn it was.

'Yes,' they chorused, and so we left the table and went upstairs to my bedroom, holding up the dress so that I didn't trip on the stairs.

It didn't take long for the three small men to have their clothes off to prove that they were ready for sex with their big cocks all at attention, sticking out from their groins. I teased them a bit more by taking my time in getting undressed until they gave out a big sigh when I was then naked and got onto the bed and had them join me there.

They didn't have to be told what I wanted, obviously having been told what the others had done whilst in bed with me. I had Sneezy and Bashful attach themselves to the nipples on my tits while Doc went down between my legs to stick his tongue inside me. It didn't take long for him to get my clit rise up to being a solid lump of flesh for his tongue to excite. I could only take so much as I would rather have had his cock inside me to give me an orgasm.

'Okay,' I said, pushing the two off my tits and squeezing Doc's head between my thighs. 'Sneezy. Lay on your back,' I told him. This he did and with him then being upside down to me, I moved down and lifted his cock upright and squatted above his thighs and slowly lowered my body down, feeling the head of his cock at the entrance to my ass. I took in a deep breath and letting go of his erection, slowly sat down on him. It was a bit painful at first in trying to get the head of his cock to pass my inside muscle there, but it finally entered me and I was able to sit right down on his thighs with his lovely cock throbbing away inside me.

I straightened my legs and then leaned back until I was on my back. 'Oww,' cried out. Sneezy sat up because with me going onto my back, his erection had been bent downwards while inside me.

'Doc, you fuck me first and Bashful, I'll have your cock in my mouth,' I said, and they were quick to move, Doc getting astride of my thighs as Bashful got across my chest.

'Get your bum out of my face, Doc,' I heard Sneezy cry out.

'Lean back on your elbows then,' Doc told him as I felt Doc's cock start to slide up into me. At the same time, I had Bashful lean over me and had the head of his cock touch my lips. I parted them and had his cock move inside my mouth. I took hold of the shaft so that he wouldn't choke me and began sucking on him as Doc began fucking me, feeling his cock rubbing Sneezy's through the thin membrane that separated the two. With him moving backwards and forwards on me. it was making me move over Sneezy's cock as I sucked on Bashful.

Oh what bliss to have three cocks inside and giving me a thrill that I never dreamed of ever having. Sneezy was not doing anything as it was my body moving on his cock that was up my ass. Doc was fucking me while I was gently chewing away at Bashful's cock in my mouth.

It was Bashful that gave me his cum before the others, it felt like the inside of my mouth had just been hit by a hot tornado being caught unawares. I just managed to close my gullet to prevent it from choking me as more cum was added, me holding his shaft firmly as he face-fucked me. I could hear him wheezing as he came to a stop, not being able to see his face that was well above me. I kept the head of his cock there as I moved his cum all round the head before swallowing it as I then got to lick the head clean and therefore have a second load to savour before swallowing it.

Only then did I release his cock from my hand and had him pull out and move down to kiss me.

You're not just a princess, but a queen and I'm just one of your abject slaves,' he said between kisses.

You're not a slave Bashful, but one of my princes with a lovely cock that gives me much pleasure whether it's in my mouth or in my pussy.'

By then, Doc was really pumping himself into me, grunting away as I felt his body go rigid and then had his cum fill me. I think that Sneezy came at the same time for it felt even bigger as it throbbed inside me. I gave out a little cry as Doc began to pull out of me and with him moving up my body, felt Sneezy's cock start to leave me too.

'Go and wash yourself, Sneezy,' I managed to say before Doc was up on my chest, squashing my tits as he kissed me, knocking Bashful to one side as he did so. I felt the bed moving as Sneezy got off and had Bashful move in between my legs and then had his tongue inside my pussy, to tease my clit as he slurped away getting Doc's cum and my own juices to suck while he was down there.

A few minutes later, Sneezy was back on the bed, pushing Doc to one side so that he could suck on a nipple and then had Doc sucking the other one with Sneezy still sucking away at my pussy.

'Three lovely well-endowed men,' I said as I stroked the heads of Doc and Sneezy, bringing my thighs together to squeeze Bashful's head before they all settled down next to me and had them stroking my body.

'Princess,' Doc began as we waited for the three of them to build up their strength again. 'Will you stay with us for Christmas?' this being only two weeks away now. 'We have great fun on Christmas Eve. We go up to the mansion every year and give the guests there a small show before we eat with the staff at their Christmas dinner. We are also given small presents plus enough food for us to eat on Christmas day.'

This gave me food for thought for Christmas wasn't that good at my sister's and so said that I would be delighted. I got more kisses from them with big smiles on their faces at me accepting this offer. I could also now feel the throbbing erections of Doc and Bashful rubbing my sides, not that of Sneezy for he was already lying between my legs kissing my lower chest but could feel his cock nestling itself at the entrance to my pussy.

So not having anal sex this time, they took turns fucking me and I then sucked on their cocks after giving me their cum. This was repeated an hour later with me then having been fucked nine times before we all fell asleep.

~~***~~

We didn't have sex in the morning upon waking up for my pussy was a bit on the sore side by having all three of them during the night and insisted that they all had a shower and with them then being nice and clean, I had my shower while they got dressed.

They had left the bedroom when I'd finished and so I got dressed in the new dress and went downstairs to cook breakfast. The other four were pleased that I was staying with them for Christmas and looked forward to me giving each one a bath at least once a week. They agreed to this knowing that after I had washed them, that I would then suck on their lovely big cocks as well as give them better meals than what they're used to.

I also wrote another letter to my sister saying that I was staying with this lovely family for Christmas and not to worry about me for I was enjoying being there with them. Little did they know that they were dwarves and I had them fucking me, though not in pairs now for I said to them that from now on, it would be one per night.

With a week being seven days, they had to take turns to be in bed with me though they still had me suck on them when I gave them a bath. So it was Doc I would have in bed with me on Sundays for him to fuck me twice before sleeping and once in the morning after waking up. The rest followed in the order of their age for the same with Dopey being with me on the Saturday night and having me three times like the others.

So over the two weeks before Christmas, I was taught the songs that I would have to be singing in the pantomime we would be doing on Christmas Eve, not knowing that when they had gone to do some shopping and posting my letter at the same time, had been in contact with two other people from the circus to join us for the pantomime. One male who would be the prince and the female being the wicked queen.

They arrived two days before Christmas Eve, though they had to sleep in the trailer as there wasn't any room in our house. We did, for those two days, run through what and how the pantomime was to be performed.

So on Christmas Eve, we trooped up to the mansion and into the grand hall where a curtain had been rigged up at one end and saw that there must have been at least twenty guests who would see us perform. I was a bag of nerves at seeing the mansion's guests as well as the owners that would be seeing us perform and the only way I could calm myself was to suck on each of the seven before we began the show.

I won't go into the story of Snow White and the Seven Dwarves as you probably know the story, but I managed to play my part and sing my songs without any hiccups and we all got a wonderful applause when we took our bows at the end. We then had dinner with the staff who would have to be working the next day in seeing to the Christmas meal of the owners and guests.

The two from the circus left us afterwards to go off to their homes for Christmas Day while we went to our house where we had a Christmas tree with all the decorations on it as well as the lounge. We had been given enough food for me to cook for our Christmas lunch and we really made pigs of ourselves in eating it.

After our lunch, we all sat in the lounge to watch the Queen's Christmas speech, after which, I was given seven small presents from beneath the tree and with me not having had the chance to get them any presents, gave them myself through the afternoon and the evening.

Naked and laying down on the big white rug in front of the fire, had four of them fuck me in the afternoon and three of them do the same in the evening. The bonus was for Dopey since it was a Saturday, and so it was him that went upstairs at bedtime with me. So not only did he fuck me in the afternoon, but he also got to fuck me that night in bed.

It was a lovely night, too. I'd had all seven of them fuck me during the day and evening and now it was time for bed. I was still naked and got up from the lovely thick carpet and took hold of Dopey's hand and led him upstairs to my bedroom. I let go of his hand when we were inside and got onto the bed as he quickly got his clothes off to let me see that he had a massive erection that swayed from side to side as he came to the bed and climbed on. It was straight to my face he came and kissed me, a hand moulding one of my tits.

'I hope it's been a Merry Christmas for you, princess,' he said.

'It has, Dopey, and with you being with me alone now is the icing on the cake,' I replied as my hand moved to take hold of his lovely cock and started rubbing it. I'm sure that the length of it was between seven and eight inches long and I could only just get my thumb and forefinger to meet as I held him in my hand. I'd already tried using both those fingers round the head before and couldn't get them to meet it was so big.

'Do you know, Dopey?' I began as my hand then took hold of his balls. 'Out of all of you, you have the biggest pair of balls.' Which was a fact, for the last time I sucked them, I couldn't get both of them into my mouth and had to suck them separately. 'I bet your father's were as big as those that you've got. He must have had a big cock, too, for you all to have big ones as well. Move down and suck my pussy first,' and pushed his head and had him move down in between my open legs.

I felt his fingers open the lips there and then had his tongue start to probe around inside me. He attacked my clit first in between darting his tongue in and out of my vagina, raising it up so that he was even able to nibble on if with his teeth. It made me squirm at the pleasure he was giving me and it wasn't long before I wanted his cock inside me.

'Now, Dopey! Now,' I gasped, my hips moving up to his face. 'Put it inside and fuck me.' I felt his wet mouth slide up my stomach until I had his head just below my tits as his cock entered and had him move down slightly to get as much of it inside me, much to my pleasure at having him fill me. It was throbbing away as my inside muscles played with it as it began moving back and forth. My legs moved up round his thighs as his hands came up to squeeze my tits as his cock pulsated away as he fucked me.

'Hold on,' I cried as I was about to have my orgasm, bucking my hips upwards and had him really ramming himself inside me. Then with a big shuddering of my body, I had my release and felt him start in giving me his cum, pumping away so that our juices joined forces and had both lots squeeze past his cock and had it all start to trickle down the crease of my bum.

His hands were really squeezing my tits hard as he came to a stop, feeling his breath come panting out of his mouth but still had his cock throbbing away inside me. He lay on top of me for several minutes before he regained his strength to lift himself up to smile up at me.

'I love you, princess,' he said, making his cock twitch inside me.

'I love you too, Dopey. Now let me suck on what has just given me such pleasure,' I said, and had him ease himself down a little, feeling his cock start to slide out of me. I gave out a little cry at losing that lovely organ and helped pull his body up over mine until I had his cock hit my chin before having the coated head move into my open mouth.

I managed to get my hand up to hold onto the shaft of his cock as I sucked away, taking in the juices from both of us that was sticking round the head. I got my other hand up to take hold of his balls and made them move about in their sac as I sucked the head of his cock until it was clean from both of our cum.

With him pulling himself out of my mouth, I said, 'The bigger of your balls is, I swear, bigger than a golf ball and it sure does hold a lot of your cum.' He sure lived up to the name I had given him for he had a silly looking smile on his face as he looked down at me.

'Will you marry me, princess?' he asked, something that I didn't expect to hear.

'I can't, Dopey. It would upset the others and I couldn't marry them too. It could cause trouble if we did,' I said. It was a crestfallen look he gave me but then slowly began to nod his head.

'You're right. It would cause a problem with them all going without being able to do what we've just done. C'est la vie.'

With that, he gave me another kiss before sliding down my body until he was between my legs and had him tonguing my pussy. He was good at that now and it wasn't long before he brought me up to another orgasm with me nearly suffocating him between my thighs as I let my cum loose for him to lick, taste and swallow.

He then came up my body a little, kissing and tonguing my navel and felt that he was once again rampant and had him push his lovely cock back up inside me. You'd think he was drilling for oil the way he fucked me, really pushing himself in as far as he could go, feeling his balls banging away at me and couldn't help the groan I gave out at the thrill and pleasure I was getting from him moving inside me

He was now able to last at least eight minutes of reaming my insides before he gave up his cum, having it shoot out as if from a cannon. This triggered me to have yet another orgasm, pushing his cum back down to coat his cock, which I then got to suck again after he had pulled out.

We must have both been exhausted after I had sucked and licked the head of his cock clean, for we then snuggled against each other and fell asleep.

~~***~~

I woke up in the morning feeling that his cock was up and hard again, pressing against my thigh and with me beginning to rub it, woke him up for him to once again push his throbbing piece of meat up into me and had him cum inside me. With him being half the size of me, we couldn't go into the sixty nine position, so after I had sucked on him, he then sucked on me before we finally got up from the bed and got him into the shower with me for us to wash each other's sex parts before getting dressed and going downstairs for me to start preparing breakfast for us all.

I couldn't help but notice at breakfast that they were all scruffy again and when I asked them if any of them had a bath since I last washed them. They should have all been named Bashful, except for Dopey, for all six heads drooped down and wouldn't look me in the eye. So I decided on a new track with them.

'As none of you have answered me, we'll start a new program. Before you can get into my bed, you will have a bath,' I began, only to have Grumpy speak first.

'Does that mean that we will get what we got last time princess?' he asked, a sly look on his face. They all, except Sleepy who yawned, looked up at me with expectations on their faces. I had to smile.

'Of course. I don't want to take a dirty dick in my mouth,' I said.

'Oh goody,' exclaimed Happy, clapping his hands. 'I'm all for that.'

'But that means I have to wait till the end of the week,' Dopey moaned.

'Serves you right for being the youngest,' Doc said. A big smile on his face as it was his turn for tonight. If I had said that they will have their bath today, they would have scrambled about in making a queue, so one every day of the week was the best bet. Besides, I could then take my time in washing what I wanted to suck. I think that there are many women who would like to be in my place here with seven men. Small that they maybe in height, but I'm sure that what they had between their legs would have had many of them drooling. I bet some men who were that way inclined would be there too. But that is just digressing.

With winter now on our doorstep so to speak, they had a rota system for who would feed the chickens and collect the eggs and for those who would be out getting more logs for the fires. They also had to do the washing up after our meals for I did enough in the cooking as well as making sure the place was kept clean.

With it being a Sunday and it was Doc's turn to share my bed and all that went with it, it surprised me that he was the first to have finished his dinner and sat there with a stupid grin on his face as I took my time in eating the meal that I had cooked but eventually, I finished and Doc was quick to leave the table and actually came round the table to pull my chair out for me to stand up.

'Time for my bath,' he said with a smug look on his face as he turned about for the others to see. So there was nothing else I could do but follow him up the stairs and into my bedroom. He was bashful in stripping his clothes off and was naked next to me as I filled the tub with hot water. His cock fully extended and bouncing about as he moved. Well the tap was running which gave me time to take my clothes off in the bedroom as he saw to the water's flow and as I returned to the bathroom, he was just getting into the bath.

So it was washing his hair first before scrubbing his back and then taking care of each leg before I got him to stand up. His cock then bounced up and down, splashing the water as it did so and stood there waiting for me to see to the washing of not only his cock and balls, but his backside too.

'This is the almost best part,' he said as I soaped his cock and balls, a job I didn't mind doing, rubbing his cock, moving the soft skin back and forth and having the eye of his cock wink at me as I did so. It didn't take long to rinse him so that his cock was then ready for me as I knelt down next to the side of the bath and took the head of his big clean cock into my mouth.

With one hand moving the skin over the hard flesh it covered, I used the other to fondle his big pair of balls as I gently chewed his cock and licked the head, making him quiver as my tongue moved over his G-string. It didn't take long before his body stiffened and I had to use both hands to stop him from choking me as he began giving me his cum. Boy what a mouthful he gave me, which I moved around in my mouth, getting a real taste of him before I swallowed it. There was only one other place that was just as good and that was having him cum inside my pussy. A pity that his body wasn't twice the size for me to be kissing him when I had an orgasm, but having him fuck me and bringing about an orgasm was something to look forward to in bed.

Releasing him from my mouth, I gave the bared flesh a kiss and helped him out of the bath to dry him off with a towel before taking his hand and moving out of the bathroom so that we could go to bed together. He kissed and thanked me for giving him a bath and then I sucked on him before moving down a little for him to suck and nibble the nipples of my tits for a little while. Then he moved further down and got in between my legs and began so suck on me. He was bloody good with his tongue and it wasn't long before I almost suffocated him as I had my first orgasm of the night with his strong tongue inside me.

It wasn't long before he was rampant again and then had the pleasure of having his throbbing cock inside me to not only give me his cum but for me to have my second orgasm. As I think I've said before, it was a pity he was so small that we couldn't move into the sixty-nine position to then suck on each other afterwards at the same time.

~~***~~

This then was the pattern for the next three months, me having Doc on Sunday nights and the others in turn during the week, them having a bath and me then sucking them off before going to bed to be fucked. I also sent off another letter to my sister saying that I would be staying with this family for quite some time yet, expecting us to part when it was time for them to return to the circus where they worked during the summer months.

It was towards the end of March that they began seeing to the clothing that they would be wearing as well as seeing that the mini bus that towed their sleeping accommodation was in good order when the subject of me was brought up.

It was two days before they were due to leave that, as we were having our dinner, Doc asked me to go with them and be a part of their group in the circus ring. They'd had a discussion earlier and it was a unanimous decision I was at a loss for words with them asking this of me. I stuttered away saying that it would be an honour to be with them but asked if the owner would accept me joining them. It was almost a chorus of them saying that the owner, one Max Turner, wouldn't refuse them as they were an integral part of the circus along with the clowns. So I thanked them and agreed to join them in the circus with me acting the part of Snow White with her seven dwarves.

The day for departure came and before we set off, Doc and Happy went up to the mansion to give them their thanks and pay the rent of the house and agreed to be there again at the end of the year. With that done, we were all in the minibus with the trailer hitched on, left the house to go to where the rest of the circus people would be meeting up.

They had already filled the trailer with lots of food though we stopped at a diner for lunch and it was eight hours after leaving the house that we turned into a big field where there were lots of trucks and trailers already gathering together. I went along with Doc and Happy to meet Max Turner, the owner, and with them telling him what they would like to do with me being a part of it, it was agreed and I was accepted as part of their group. It was then back to the trailer for us to have dinner.

Now the trailer was as long as it was allowed to be whilst on the road and inside, the front half was just one massive bed. The middle part held the kitchen as well as the toilet and shower and also was the door that opened outward. The back end was the dining area where the table could be lowered down afterwards and the two cushioned benches either side could be pulled out to make another bed for sleeping on. This was where I would be sleeping with two of the men, who would later, change places every night, so I would have a different two each time to sleep and have sex with.

I lost track of the names of all the people of the circus that I was introduced to, only remembering what they did within the circus. The clowns, not dressed up as yet. The ring master, the lion tamer, the trapeze artists, the horse riders and others, some who saw to the erection of the big top as well as the staff who did various other things.

Dinner was to be early as it would be an early start in the morning to move off to where the first show was to be given. Small as the kitchen was in the trailer, with some help, it didn't take long to cook and serve dinner, everyone mucking in to help by laying the table and then seeing to the washing up afterwards. While the latter was being done, the table was lowered down and the bed for that end of the trailer was set up for the night.

Now with it being my first night in the trailer, I had no choice as to who would be sleeping with me. Whether they rolled dice or used straw, I never found out, but I finished up with having Bashful and Sleepy in our bed at the rear end of the trailer.

Needless to say that I sucked on one whilst being fucked by the other and an hour later it was reversed. But that was all that we did that first night, much to my chagrin, for everybody had to be up early to see to the raising of the big top. I forgot to mention that the circus also had four elephants, and they would be then used in the raising of the big top. Each were put on one corner and one of the long ropes were put around their trunks and on the order to move, did so in moving backwards and therefore pulling the ropes that lifted the big top up to its full height to be secured by the men inside.

With the big top in place, the insides were then filled with the seating arrangements whilst others saw to the fixing on the trapeze artistes cables etc. The whole of which took up most of the day before it was then ready once the ring was then covered with sawdust.

I was trembling when it was time for my first introduction as a member of the cast. A small trailer had been covered with different types of material for me to then sit up on top and have my seven dwarves getting into position to pull me out into the ring.

Doc was the leader at the head of the trailer with the other six pulling along at the sides as we finally made our entrance into the ring. The Master of Ceremonies', when it was our turn, introduced us as Snow White and her seven dwarves, and into the ring we went with them beginning to sing that famous song.

'Heigh Ho! Heigh Ho! It's off to work we go,' they sang as they pulled the cart into the ring to the applause of the crowd that were now seated at our first show of the year. The seven of them looked grand in their costumes as they pulled the cart into and took a turn round the ring, singing away as I waved to the audience.

It was exhilarating to wave to the crowd and almost had an orgasm at the way I felt being paraded as Snow White, whose copy of dress I was wearing. When it got to the point of them then playing and tumbling around with the clowns, all I had to do was clap my hands like the audience. To tell the truth, I really enjoyed it and was somewhat dismayed when my cart was then pulled back out of the ring for the lion tamer to do his tricks as well as the elephants followed by the horses.

Such was the thrill I'd had by being in the ring with my seven small men. When we were back outside, Doc climbed up to where I was sitting and had him fuck me to give me the orgasm that had been building up inside me, not withstanding having him cum inside me at the same time. I was delirious in the pleasure of both and couldn't wait until it was our turn again to enter the ring. I had Grumpy fuck me the second time and after the final parade had Happy fuck me. Needless to say, that the two who shared the bed that night were Sleepy and Dopey. Both of them having the rampant cocks that I not only loved sucking on but having them up inside as they fucked me to round off one of the best days of my life.

It was a lovely first night for me as was all the other nine, for we did ten evening performances and nine in the afternoons before we moved on to another town. It was almost in a circle that we moved from town to town to finish up the season at one that was closest to the town we had started from.

I wrote a couple of letters to my sister telling her that I had found a job in a circus, but didn't say exactly what I was doing.

So for nearly seven months, I played the part of Snow White and later, every night, was fucked by two of them as they changed places in our trailer so that they each had their turn in doing so. I lost count of how many times each of them fucked me, me loving each and every one of them with their big and throbbing cocks being pushed up into me and then having the extra pleasure of sucking on them afterwards. Mind you, they sucked and tongued me too.

It was at this last stop that a man from the audience collared Doc and asked him if he and the other six, plus me, would put on a pantomime at his theatre in the very near future. The one rider he had was if I could sing. Doc assured him that I had a perfect voice but that he would have to ask us all if we would agree. The man agreed and we would see him the following day for his answer.

Doc was all bubbly at dinner in the trailer and when it was over, told us what he'd been asked and if we all would agree to doing this pantomime. It was a resounding yes from the others and it even woke up Sleepy.

'Being on a stage has given me a hard on,' he exclaimed. I even wet my panties when he said that, so I got up from the table and pulled him down to the other end of the trailer and got him to sit down on the edge of the bed there. I was on my knees and I opened up the front of his trousers and pulled out his enlarged and pulsating cock and gave the half exposed head a kiss before taking it into my mouth, sucking on it as my hand moved the soft flesh up and down over the hard muscle it covered.

He gave out a groan and leaned back as I sucked and excited him with me also gently chewing his cock, which I loved sucking when it wasn't up inside me. With it firmly in my hand being moved up and down and with my tongue teasing the G-string, soon had him gasping and felt his thighs tighten as he began to unload his balls of the cum that then erupted into my mouth for me to move around, getting the taste of him before swallowing it.

As his cock started to soften up, I released it and stowed it back inside his trousers and with him then sitting up, pulled me close and kissed me, thanking me for doing what I had just done. I then called Doc to come and sit down, letting Sleepy move off the bed to let Doc have his turn. His cock head was a bright red when I pulled it out from his trousers and pushed the foreskin down with my lips as I took his throbbing cock into my mouth to suck and chew. It didn't take long before I had him give me his cum to savour before swallowing it.

I got another three to come and let me suck on them leaving Sneezy and Bashful till last for it was their turn to be in bed with me that night and would see to them then. It didn't take long for the table to be removed and our bed set up, me leaving them to do this as I took off my clothes to be naked to get on the bed. They were quick to get their clothes off and join me. Literally as well, for Bashful was soon pushing his cock into me, feeling it throbbing away as he moved in and had me drooling as he fucked me with his lovely big piece of meat. Having already sucked on five of them, my own body was desperate for release and had an orgasm almost immediately with having his cock plough my meadow, my legs tight up to his waist as I bucked beneath him.

Such was his need as well, he soon came inside me, feeling his cum coating my insides before he came to a panting stop, his hands then moulding my tits as he kissed my lower chest.

'I love you, princess,' he whispered when he lifted his head up, resting his chin between my tits.

'I love you too, Bashful. As much as I do Sneezy who is bouncing up and down waiting for his turn,' I told him. Which was true, for Sneezy's cock was moving up and down like an angled pendulum.

'Bugger him,' said Bashful.

'I'll get him buggering you if you don't give him his turn,' I told him. That shifted him, making him slide off my body to finish up sitting on the floor and having Sneezy trample on him as he threw himself up onto me. His cock got squashed between us as he kissed me before sliding back down and felt his big cock drop between my thighs that were open for him. With his hands gripping my waist, he heaved himself up and had him enter me. What bliss it was to have another pulsating cock slide back up inside me. I held his head in my hands as he moved himself inside as he fucked me, my legs up in the air to let him get as much of himself into me, but sadly, he was soon cumming inside me before I was anywhere near me having another orgasm.

While Sneezy was unloading his cum into me, Bashful had gotten back up onto the bed and I had his still hard cock brush my lips which I opened and took the wet head into my mouth for me to suck off both his cum and some of my orgasmic juices. In the meantime, Sneezy pulled out of me and moved up the bed and found that I had a big mouth for he then poked the head of his cock up against Bashful's cock and had the head in my mouth at the same time. This was a first, and also the last, for I nearly choked at having two cock heads being pushed into my mouth and had to push the pair of them back so that their cocks then slapped against my face as I did so.

I grabbed both of their cocks and really squeezed them in my hands. 'Don't do that again,' I said to Sneezy, coughing as I spoke, 'or that will be the last time I suck you.'

'Sorry, princess. I thought you might like two at the same time,' he said.

'Little boys maybe, but not cocks of your sizes,' I said, just before I sneezed.

'Bless you,' they said in unison as I pulled up a corner of the sheet to wipe my nose.

'Okay. Now settle down and let's get to sleep and you can then, in the morning, have me again,' I said, pushing them away for them to settle down alongside me, pulling the bed covers up for us to go to sleep.

~~***~~

Needless to say that they both had their oats in the morning while I had two orgasms and got both of them to take turns licking me out of what they had put inside me along with my juices.

Because of the way that I had berated them that night, they both helped me see to breakfast after we had dressed and all of them were in high spirits with the thought of us actually going to do a pantomime on a proper theatre later.

Doc got in touch with the owner and agreed to us performing and got the date that we were required to visit his theatre for a week of rehearsals. That soon came round and we presented ourselves there and were soon told what we could and couldn't do with the theatre having children present. This was understood and it really was to see if I could sing the songs required and that the dwarves behaved themselves.

On stage, Molly Stiggers was the epitome of what the wicked queen looked like. Her best bits saying that famous dialogue of "Mirror, mirror on the wall, who is the fairest of them all." And then giving the poisoned apple to Snow White upon finding out that she was the most beautiful of them all.

Prince Charming was a lovely looking man, and with him standing there, wearing a cod piece inside his trousers, really looked a dream, but I found out later that his dick was much smaller than all of the seven dwarves. I only know this by actually catching him in his dressing room with him not wearing his cod piece to. I also found out that he was gay, so he was a no go to my mind.

We did our prancing about the stage, my seven little men being the real stars, and were ready when the time came for us to do the show in front of an audience. I still, in the meantime, had all seven of them fuck me at their night turns and I continued to suck on their lovely cocks that had been up inside me.

It appeared that the show was successful with me at the end being kissed awake by Prince Charming and then leaving the stage arm in arm as we were bid farewell by the seven little men. We did this show for two weeks with the seven of them getting oats and me taking it in when they fucked me as well as getting some of my own juices when I sucked on them after pulling out of me.

I refused to take the pay from Doc after we had finished our time in the theatre, telling him that it should be shared amongst the others as they looked after me all the time. This brought sniggers from most of them for it was really me that looked after them in more than one way.

It was then back to their winter cottage where we slipped into the same routine as before with having one per night in bed with me, but only after I gave all seven a bath, sucking on their cocks in the process, with them not being able to have a bath in the little trailer. This was on the Sunday, so it was Doc in my bed for the night. I drooled at the mouth as he got onto the bed, standing there with his massive cock sticking out in front of him. I opened up my legs and had him drop forward and had him ram his cock up inside me, thrilling me at having him once again moving himself inside me

I had my orgasm almost immediately with his head buried below my tits, seeing his ass move up and down as he fucked me. In spite of having had me suck on his cock when bathing him a few hours previously, he still gave me an incredible amount of his cum, feeling it shoot out of his cock as he came to a panting halt.

It took him several minutes to regain his breath and pull out of me, only to come up and lean over me so that I could suck on his lovely cock. Not only getting the residue of his cum but my juices too for me to move both around in my mouth before swallowing it all. He couldn't stop kissing me when he moved a little way down on me.

'Oh princess.' he murmured between kisses. 'The day of your arrival was a godsend, for I've never seen the others so happy having you with us. Even Grumpy seems to have mellowed and Dopey cannot stop praising you. We all love you, especially having a night in bed with you.'

'I love you too, Doc, and all the others,' I said as he slipped even further down so that he could suck on my nipples, 'doing what you are doing now as well as having each of you inside me every night.'

He carried on for a while at his sucking of my tits before going right down to tongue me. It wasn't long before I began begging him to fuck me again and so a minute or two later, he rose up for me to see that his cock was as big as ever before he plunged back into me again.

What bliss to have all my inside nerves giving out their tingles the way his cock slid back and forth and had to hold his head as I began to buck myself beneath him as I began to have my second orgasm and also feel him cumming inside me at the same time.

It wasn't long after this that we fell asleep as we cuddled each other.

~~***~~

I had him fuck me in the morning after we had woken up and us then, having finished, having a shower together before drying ourselves and getting dressed to go downstairs to start getting breakfast for all of us.

That was the pattern for the two weeks before Christmas Eve, having each of them in my bed at night for sex between us as well as the morning fuck before having a shower. Then with that day arriving, we had the two people we had the year before, join us to go up to the mansion to give our little pantomime for the owners and their guests. Of course we had our Christmas Eve dinner there with the staff afterwards, before returning to our cottage down in the woods.

The Christmas tree had been erected a week earlier and now it had a bundle of presents that we had bought for each other from our return from the circus beneath it. The other present I had for them all was letting them fuck me in the lounge with the others watching, though this was spread out during the day, not wanting to get sore by having them fuck me one after another.

I had sent a Christmas card to my sister with a letter saying that I would be staying with my friends from now on and not to worry about me. They couldn't send me one or contact me for I didn't give them the address of where my seven little men lived. I was happy being with them and also went with them later in the year to perform in the circus again.

It had been a blessing in disguise with me leaving that man's car and stumbling into the woods for me to finish up where I was now, and it looked as though we would be spending quite a few years together with me having unlimited sex which we all enjoyed.

The End

Here is a preview of another story you may enjoy:

Amy Redek

Farell

Hot Romance Erotica

'It was a dark and stormy night and the lightening crashed and the thunder flashed,' I began before being interrupted by a bright seven-year-old girl.

'Excuse me, Mr. Farrell,' her right arm held up high, 'but shouldn't that be the lightning flashed and the thunder crashed?'

'Quite right, my young Miss. I changed the words to see if you were paying attention,' which proved that at least one was. This was becoming my party piece as I was always invited to the birthday parties of my niece and nephew and as the end of the party was nigh, I would always be asked to tell a ghost story. The floor would be cleared and we would only have the light of a solitary candle on the mantel piece behind me as the children sat in a semi-circle before me, holding hands. So in the gloom of the room with just this single flickering light that didn't show my features, I had to make the most of the story with the tones of my voice. They liked it when it was deep and sonorous to try and portray that somewhere outside of our circle was a mysterious and threatening presence.

One year, I didn't begin with those words and I had cries of dismay, so ever since, I've had to begin my stories the same way. They understood these words whether it be around an old house alone in the middle of the moors, or a castle perched high on a cliff edge with the seas crashing and rolling against the sharp jagged rocks that had seen many ships founder. They could imagine the single flashing light high up in the castle, luring a ship to its destruction on the rocks below.

These were pictures they could conjure up in their mind's eye as I described the wind and the way that it talks to man, bird and beast. This was the beginning to their story and it was not to be left out though the critics say that a book should never open with these lines, but it was the way that my critics who sat before me all wanted it to begin.

But my own story for you really started with it being quite the opposite, though if I ever got to tell it to the children, it would have to be different. Spring had arrived and the sun was shining and all seemed right with the world. My name is Michael Farrell and I'm slightly overweight for my height of six foot if taken with my being thirty-two years of age. I have light blue eyes, clean shaven, average features and have brown to black coloured hair which is of no value to the story but just helps to fill up the picture for you to see me.

I live alone in a cottage, of which there are twelve in what is known as Meadows Lane that leads nowhere from the lane at the top. This top lane, or road is one of those nightmare thoroughfares that only has passing areas about two hundred yards apart. Not lay-bys but just bits of ground where the hedge has been crushed over the years and were now just bare patches of earth that were full of mud and icy water during the winter. Many's the time you can hear the honking of horns as two vehicles meet and neither want to reverse to clear the way. It is usually the one with a female inside that finally gives way and makes the tricky job of reversing round a blind bend to be able to pull into the hedge lined gap.

This was the road at the top of my lane and it had just a small pub and one shop that sold a lot of nothing, and to complete this part of the village, there were six cottages either side of these two public places. These were all on the right as we came out and turned left from Meadows Lane because the land opposite and onto which my cottage backed, was Meadows Farm.

It was over a quarter of a mile before we came to the stables on the right and this was directly opposite another lane that ran in the same direction as the one I lived in. Now this would show the ingenuity of the district's planning many years ago, because it bounded the other side of Meadows Farm and that my lane was called Meadows Lane, they named this one by just dropping the letter S. Brilliant thinking on someone's part. This lane too had twelve cottages and so it was almost a mirror image to mine if one could look down from above.

Now at the bottom of the two lanes and of the farm in between was what locally known as the cliffs. A misnomer if ever there was one like calling our hamlet a village. Our cliffs were about twenty foot high and as the land and soil slowly broke away with wind and rain, they became slopes that ran down to a narrow pebbled beach, if I could even call it that. Though the land of the farm was flat where the farmhouse stood, it rose up towards the sea end but rolled down on either side to where the lanes were, so from where I lived, I couldn't see the lane on the other side of these fields because of this small hill.

I know, I know, you're getting impatient for me to start the story but I had to give you the lay out and topography of the place first and you'll understand why in a minute. Now I'll get to the problem I caused our postie, postman to you townies, his name by the way is Pat. Well, that is what everybody calls him like they call our village Toy Town. We don't have a Noddy but we do have a Big Ears, but due to the size of the fellow, no one has ever dared call him that. Built like a brick…, er, outhouse, with arms and shoulders that many a tree would be proud to have limbs like that. He was much in demand at harvest time because he could pitch fork even the most soggiest of hay bales to toss it over twenty feet high onto the hay wagon.

But the problem I caused our postman was of my surname Farrell, because there was another man of that name in the opposite lane, only his Christian name was Nicholas. When we did eventually meet, it became Mick and Nick, mine coming first alphabetically. What compounded postman Pat's problem was none of the cottages had numbers or names and he delivered by the surname on the letter, so sometimes I got Nick's and he got mine if the writer dropped the letter S. Also I think Pat had an eye problem to tell the difference between the two letters of our Christian names.

It was a joke when it first happened as I got a letter that was meant for Nick and so I took a walk along the cliffs and over the hill to hand deliver it myself for which he opened a bottle of beer as a thank you. Then another day he delivered one to me and I reciprocated with a bottle of beer and a chat. Now this would happen three, maybe four times a year so we both now always kept a few bottles of beer available in the pantry as payment.

It was on this glorious spring morning that Pat delivered one for Nick to my cottage, so after I had my breakfast and washed up and put the things away decided to take over his letter. I put it in my jacket pocket and went out into the garden but stopped as I looked at the sorry state of my roses. I saw that they could do with a bit of nutrient about now if I wanted a good showing this year, so decided to call in at the stables first to order some manure.

I walked up my lane and turned left and gave a wave to Dave, the pub landlord as he was seeing to his weekly delivery by the draymen. I ambled along the lane, keeping one ear cocked for the sound of any approaching vehicle from either direction, but as we are such a way off the beaten track, we don't get that many. I called in at the stables and spoke to the head lad; lad? He was nearly double my age and agreed to drop a couple of bags off at my cottage though I stressed that only when there was time and not to rush, which was a bit of a joke because nobody rushed in Toy Town.

With the manure ordered, I then went down the lane to Nick's cottage and I called out as I entered the garden but only got silence as a response. I went round to his back door which was never locked and went in, calling out his name again. The kitchen was clean and tidy but still no Nick. I went and felt the tea cloth and found that it was damp which told me he'd eaten and washed up. I went to his pantry and took out a bottle of beer and put it in the middle of the table so that it was a reminder of what he owed me as I propped his letter up against it.

I went out closing the door and down through his garden for the walk along the cliffs back to my place. It certainly was a pleasure to walk through the grass and feel the first hint of warmth from the sun on my back so I took my jacket off and slung it over my shoulder, enjoying the slight breeze coming off the sea and I could hear what I thought were larks as I got near the top of the small hill.

It was by looking up into the sky and not looking where I was putting my feet that I tripped and went sprawling flat down on my stomach, and as I raised my head, came face to face with Nick. There, in the grass, eyes half closed and the mouth fixed in a rictus of a grin, a foot away from me was Nick's head…

If you enjoyed this sample, look for **Farell.**

Here's another preview of another book you may also enjoy:

BOOK 1

ELUSIVE BILLIONAIRE ROMANCE SERIES

SHYLA STARR

"I want to know who the hell is responsible for this mess!" boomed Hendrick from the front of the boardroom.

Silence filled the room as all the top people in the company stared at Hendrick in awe. They knew he wasn't the kind of guy to be messed with. Considering the company had just been charged with federal and criminal charges for dumping industrial waste into the Arctic Ocean, they knew it was best to stay silent.

"I return from vacation to find the prosecutor in my office to tell me that a company that I built from the ground up to help humanity is being accused of filling the ocean with waste! Waste??" He screamed across the table, his face turning an angry red. Hendrick stopped for a moment to compose himself and looked at each person at the table, assessing their worth.

"Pray it was not one of you frontrunners that made the decision to handle the waste of the company in this manner. Now go, and I expect reports hourly about how we are making this right and where waste should be going from now on."

Everyone got up from the table quickly and filtered out of the room. Hendrick watched them all leave and turned to his right-hand man, Geoffrey, the CEO of the company.

"Tell me you didn't know."

A broad-shouldered man, Geoffrey held an imposing frame that fit well with the red beard that made him appear like a Viking. He was incredibly loyal and a great asset to the company.

"You have known me your whole life, Hendrick. I'm sure you know I had nothing to do with dumping waste into the ocean. The person in charge of a decision like that is one of your minions."

"How is it that the owner and CEO of a company had no idea that his own company has been poisoning the ocean?"

"Someone down the line obviously felt it would save the company a lot of money."

Hendrick snorted, "Ya and no one would ever find out that the Arctic Ocean was suddenly polluted? My god, they have vessel numbers and everything, it was our guys to be sure, so how do I not know about it?"

"The prosecutors are doing their investigation and so are we. I can guarantee that we will find out who is responsible before anyone else does."

"I'm being prosecuted, Geoffrey! They think I knew about this madness."

"Look, you didn't know and they can't prove that you did. You will have your day in court and they will simply have to let it go. They can't pull evidence from thin air so you're safe."

Hendrick went to the side table by the grand picture window. He poured them both a glass of bourbon, handing one to Geoffrey.

"I built this company because I believed in a vision and now our reputation is being smeared. All the while I'm off doing fundraisers and charity events while some asshole is destroying the ocean under my name."

"Hendrick, it's your job to do those things. That's how money is raised and you don't need to be at the company all the time. That's my job, to handle the bullshit. I apologize that this issue slipped through my fingers. I assure you it will be handled. We certainly won't be dealing with such an issue as this in the future."

They clinked glasses before Hendrick took a strong gulp of his.

"What do you suggest for damage control?"

Geoffrey faced the window and looked outside, taking a moment to collect his thoughts. He took a sip of bourbon, turning to face Hendrick.

"Africa."

"Excuse me?"

"I've looked into some options and we need huge PR points right now. Not only that but Africa needs people to help build a school and a hospital in one of its most impoverished places."

"And this is going to work?"

"Brilliantly. We are going to give them a ton of money while you are going to fly there and get your hands dirty to show the world what your company really stands for."

"After this mess, it's the least I can do."

"Good, because you leave on Monday."

If you enjoyed this sample, look for **Suspicion** by **Shyla Starr**.

Also by this Author

The Painted Sword

Cruise Control

Wild Pleasures

Lending My Beloved

Lady of Cuckolds

Lady of Pleasure

Lady Magenta

Sexually Overdosed

Meeting My Fancy Dear

Prison Sex Slave

Chasing A Shadow

The Hostel

The Island

Thirst for Drugs and Pleasure

Forgotten Identity

Grey Memories

Chronos: Time Machine

The Hard Bomber

Honeymoon Abduction

The Yacht Sins

Summer at the Villa

Practice Makes Perfect

Stranger Danger

Following Father's Footsteps

The Square Circle

The Wizard of Kos

Out in the Real World

Me, Carol and Raoul

Under the Mistletoe

Loving Rhett

Farell

From the Author

Check my page on Amazon and my blog for Updates and interesting info.

Author Central – http://www.amazon.com/Amy-Redek/e/B00A48NQ72
Author Blog – http://amy-redek.awesomeauthors.org/

If you enjoyed any of my books then please share the love and click like on my books in Amazon.

If you write me a review and send me an email I will send you a free book, or many.
(Just know that these emails are filtered by my publisher.)

Good news is always welcome.

One Last Thing, For Kindle Readers...

When you turn the page, Kindle will give you the opportunity to rate this book and share your thoughts on Facebook and Twitter. If you enjoyed my writings, would you please take a few seconds to let your friends know about it? Because... when they enjoy they will be grateful to you and so will I.

Thank You!

Amy Redek
amy_redek@awesomeauthors.org

About the Author

George Eliot was a famous writer, though at the time, only male authors were recognised. It was in fact the pen name of Mary Ann Evans, a female.

When I started writing, I thought that if a woman could use a male name, why, with me being male, why couldn't I use the name of a female? Though to be different, I made my writer's name from an anagram of my real name.

I wasn't the brightest spark in my school days and it was only while being in the Merchant Navy did I self-educate myself. That being mostly literature, classical music and artists, like Tolstoy, Chopin and Rembrandt. After leaving the navy, I had several jobs, finishing up by being a working boss using my own maxim that 'Management is the art of delegation.'

It's when I became self-employed that I began to write, though sadly, not many of my books can be published because of certain laws that forbid certain aspects of life. This never fazed me for I was really writing just to please myself having a wide range of the human psych.

Having written ninety stories, my only aim now is to reach one hundred. I give thanks to the publishers for at least putting some of my efforts out for others to enjoy as much as I did in the writing of them.